A Note to Parents

Read to your child...

★ Reading aloud is one of the best ways to develop your child's love of reading. Older readers still love to hear stories.

★ Enthusiasm is contagious. Read with feeling. Show your child that reading is fun.

★ Take time to answer questions your child may have about the story. Linger over pages that interest your child.

...and your child will read to you.

★ Do not correct every word your child misreads.
Say, "Does that make sense? Let's try it again."

★ Praise your child as he progresses. Your encouraging words will build his confidence.

You can help your Level 2 reader.

★ Keep the reading experience interactive. Read part of a sentence, then ask your child to add the missing word.

★ Read the first part of a story, then ask your child, "What's going to happen next?"

★ Give clues to new words. Say, "This word begins with b and ends in ake, like rake, take, lake."

★ Ask your child to retell the story using her own words.

★ Use the five Ws: WHO is the story about? WHAT happens? WHERE and WHEN does the story take place? WHY does it turn out the way it does?

Most of all, enjoy your reading time together!

Library of Congress Cataloging-in-Publication Data

Teitelbaum, Michael.
Trucking across America / written by Michael Teitelbaum
    p. cm. – (All-star readers. Level 2)
"Tonka."
ISBN-13: 978-0-7944-1000-1
ISBN-10: 0-7944-1000-6
I. Title. II. Series.

PZ7.T233Tr2006   2005044353

Trucking Across America

by Michael Teitelbaum
illustrated by Thomas LaPadula

All-Star Readers™

Reader's Digest Children's Books™

Pleasantville, New York • Montréal, Québec

I drive a truck. It's a big rig, an 18-wheeler. I'm about to set off on a cross-country trip.

My truck is carrying cargo from the East Coast all the way to the West Coast.

It's time to hit the highway. There is so much to see as I look out my window.

A new shopping mall is being built
next to the highway. A powerful
bulldozer is moving a big mound
of dirt.

The mighty backhoe is digging a deep hole with its huge metal claw.

Here comes a flatbed truck.
It's carrying a big load of lumber.
That's one strong truck!

Now I'm out in farm country. A shiny tanker truck stops at a farm.

Milk is stored in the truck's big tank. The milk moves through a hose into the tanker truck.

11

A yellow tractor is at work. Its tires are big. Its engine is strong. The farmer uses it to plow his field.

There's a pickup truck. It's carrying big bales of hay in its bed.

I drive past a big auto plant.
Look, there's a huge car carrier.

It's being loaded with brand-new cars. The carrier will bring the cars to people all over the country.

New houses are being built on that hillside. A concrete mixer is pouring concrete for the foundations.

The loader scoops up rocks and
dirt to make room for the houses.
Then the loader dumps them into
a dump truck.

Up ahead, there's been an accident!
The ambulance races to the rescue!
Its siren screams. Its lights flash!

Luckily, no one is hurt. The tow truck arrives. It tows the car with its big hook.

I'm in the mountains now.
It's snowing!

A snowplow clears the road with its big blade.

There's a sport-utility vehicle.
We call that an SUV. Its big tires
really grip the road.

The road is steep and winding now.
I use my brakes to control my speed.

The road over there is being paved. There's a grader. It uses its long blade to smooth out the bridge's roadway.

Here comes a steamroller.
It's very heavy. Its roller flattens
out the blacktop.

In a city, I pass a building on fire.
The fire truck is on the scene.

Water blasts from the fire fighters'
hoses. Other fire fighters climb tall
ladders to rescue people.

At last, I arrive on the West Coast.
It's time to unload my truck.

Here comes a forklift. Its two
metal arms can carry all kinds
of heavy loads.

A tall crane lifts the empty
container off my truck.
It rises high into the air.

Soon the crane will place a new
container onto my truck. Then
I'll be ready for the trip home.

Words are fun!

Try these simple activities. All you need are colored markers, a sheet of paper, and your imagination!

———————— ★ ————————

1. You read about lots of cool vehicles in this story. Now draw your favorite truck or vehicle. What does it look like? Does it have wheels? Does it fly? Does it travel on water?

2. Put these events into the order in which they happen in the story:

- **a. a forklift empties the truck's cargo**
- **b. a snowplow clears the road**
- **c. a fire truck helps put out a fire**
- **d. a tanker truck fills up with milk at a farm**

3. Find the two words in each line that rhyme.

truck	**track**	**luck**
plow	**now**	**tow**
while	**wheel**	**seal**
tire	**higher**	**tore**
crane	**crate**	**rain**

4. The truck driver in this story passes by mountains, cities, and farms. If you could drive a truck, where would you like to visit? Draw a picture showing where you would go.

5. Which word means the opposite of the word on the left?

- **a. first (fast, last, under)**
- **b. new (short, easy, old)**
- **c. powerful (weak, quick, large)**
- **d. shiny (round, dull, flat)**
- **e. long (colorful, smooth, short)**
- **f. high (low, deep, thick)**

6. Unscramble each of these words to find the name of a vehicle from this story:

- **a. X M E R I**
- **b. A R D E L O**
- **c. T R O F I K F L**
- **d. N E C A R**